CATFISH

CATFISH

Edith Thacher Hurd

Pictures by Clement Hurd

THE VIKING PRESS

NEW YORK

Once there was a cat named Catfish.

Catfish lived with a man named Mush Mouth.

Catfish and Mush Mouth
lived in a little town named
Nevermind.

When Catfish was a little cat
he rode his tricycle
    up and down
    round and round
the little town of Nevermind.
"Be careful," Mush Mouth said.
"You'll get smashed up."

And Catfish did.

WHOP!

Catfish's tricycle was just a
hunk of junk.

But when Christmas came
Catfish got a bicycle.
This bicycle was a
    high-speed
    low-speed
    stop-and-go
    whiz-bang
    bicycle.

"Be careful,"
Mush Mouth said.
But Catfish
wasn't careful.
Not at all.
WHIZ!
Catfish rode that
high-speed low-speed bicycle
all over the town of Nevermind.
"That cat rides his bicycle too fast,"
said Mr. Fix-It-Fine, the Mayor. "Get him out of town."

"Cat, get out of town!" roared Mighty Mince Meat,
the Chief of Police of the town of Nevermind.

So Catfish rode his bicycle right out of town.

Catfish rode his bicycle until he came

to the shining tracks the train ran on.

"Choo-choo, to Kalamazoo,
  all the way through to Kalamazoo,"
purred Catfish, as he rode his bicycle
between the shining tracks the train ran on.

                    Then Catfish heard a whistle!

WHOO-OO-OO

Catfish heard a whistle, whistling.

Whoo-oo-oo!

Catfish heard an engine puffing.
Puff-puff-puffing down the track.

Away went Catfish
with the fast train
whistling behind him.

WHOO-OO-OO

The engineer,
the fireman,
and all the people shouted,
"Get off the track, you crazy cat.
We're going through to Kalamazoo,
all the way through to Kalamazoo."

But Catfish kept on riding,
riding,
riding,
UNTIL . . .

The engine caught him
on the cowcatcher.
And it carried him through,
all the way through
to Kalamazoo,
riding on the cowcatcher.

Now Catfish didn't have a bicycle.

Catfish didn't have a tricycle.

But when Christmas came

Catfish got . . .

a MOTORCYCLE!

It was a beautiful red motorcycle.
It made a lot of noise.
Pop! Bang! Bang!
Nobody in all the town of Nevermind
liked that pop-bang motorcycle.
Nobody but Catfish,
and Catfish liked it very much.

Catfish

got a helmet.

. He got

some goggles.

BANG POP POP BANG POP BANG

Bang! Pop!
Pop! Bang! Pop!
Speeding
round and round,
Catfish
rode very fast
all over town.

BANG POP

"Oh, that Catfish,"
said Mighty Mince Meat.
"I'll get that cat this time."
BUT . . .

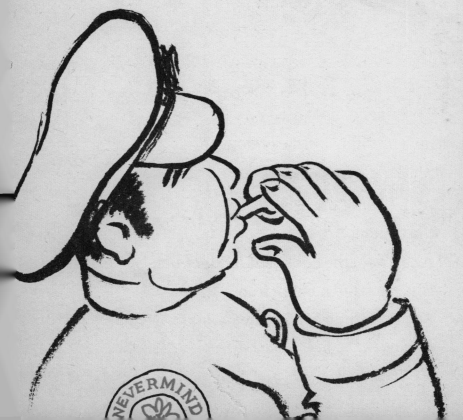

Just then the fire alarm went off.

Whee-ee-ee!

Away went Siren Red,

the fire chief.

Away went the hook-and-ladder truck.

Out came the pumper truck.

And up in front of all of these was CATFISH!

Racing to the fire.

Siren Red was mad,

so mad that he turned the hose on Catfish.

And the house almost burned down.

Now **everyone** in Nevermind was mad at Catfish.

Mr. Fix-It-Fine, Siren Red,

Mighty Mince Meat, and even Mush Mouth.

"That's a no-good cat," said **everyone** in Nevermind.

So Mush Mouth took away
Catfish's beautiful red motorcycle.

He gave it to some silly cat
who didn't even know how to ride it.

Now Catfish didn't have a motorcycle.

Catfish didn't have a bicycle.

Catfish didn't have a tricycle.

Catfish walked around
and round the town
with his tail hanging down behind him.

"What I need," said Catfish, "is a
nice, new,
bright, new, shiny,
very, very fast
AUTOMOBILE!"

Catfish thought and thought. Where could
a little cat like Catfish get the money to buy
an automobile?

Just then a beautiful big car drove by.
Inside the car was the president of the biggest
bank in Nevermind.

Catfish snapped his fingers.

Catfish twirled his whiskers.

Away went Catfish to try to get some money from

the president of the biggest bank in Nevermind.

"NO!" the president shouted.

"Get out of here!

I don't lend money to just any cat in town."

Poor
Catfish!
Out he went.
And that's
when it
happened.

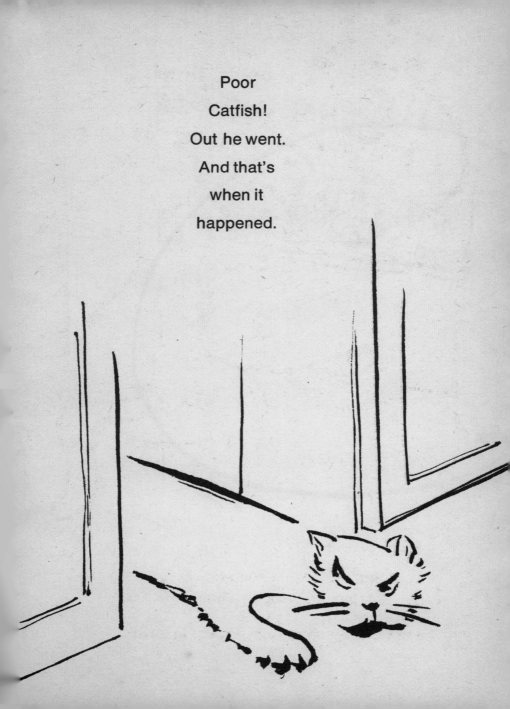

Two Fat Cats drove up in a fine French car.

"Stand back, small cat," they hissed.

"This here is a holdup."

"Stick 'em up!" they shouted.

"This here is a holdup."

Quick as a wink the president rang the alarm
for Mighty Mince Meat, the Chief of Police.
But Mighty Mince Meat disappeared when
that burglar alarm went off.

So the Fat Cats took the cash.

One bag,

two bags,

three bags,

four.

The Fat Cats took four bags of gold and silver.

They fired three shots

as they roared away in their fine French car.

   Bang!

   Bang!

   Bang!

Catfish felt a whisker fly.

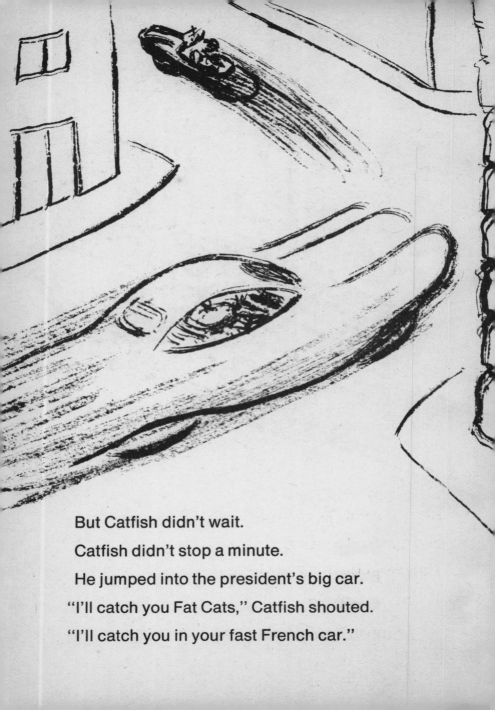

But Catfish didn't wait.

Catfish didn't stop a minute.

He jumped into the president's big car.

"I'll catch you Fat Cats," Catfish shouted.

"I'll catch you in your fast French car."

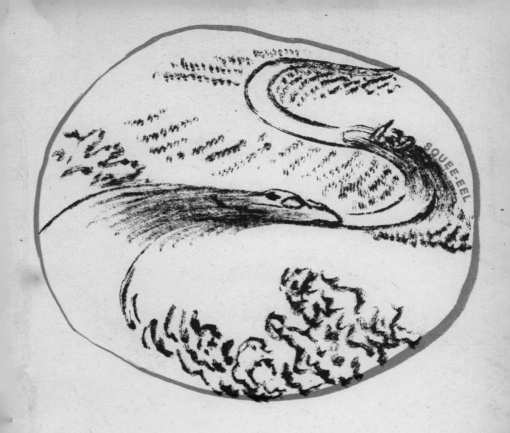

Away the Fat Cats went,

one hundred miles an hour.

They roared around the corner

   on two wheels—

   SQUEE-EEL!

The Fat Cats fired three more shots.

Catfish felt another whisker fly.

Then Catfish saw where those two Fat Cats
were going.
Catfish heard a whistle blowing.

The train going through

to Kalamazoo

was coming down the track.

What a CONGLOMERATION!

What a mess!

Fat Cats, gold, and silver.

And that beautiful French car.

Mr. Fix-It-Fine and Siren Red

came roaring on the hook-and-ladder truck.

The president came in Mush Mouth's little tiny car.

Last of all came Mighty Mince Meat
in his big Police Chief's car.

"Oh, oh," cried the president. "I've lost all my money, all my gold and silver. The Fat Cats took it all."

"I beg your pardon, sir," said Catfish.

"Here are your Fat Cats."

Then he opened the door of the president's

big car. "And here is your gold and silver."

"Who is this cool cat?" the president shouted.

"Just my little Catfish," Mush Mouth said.

"And **my** friend," said Mighty Mince Meat.

"Fastest cat in town," said Siren Red.

"Bravest cat in town," said Mr. Fix-It-Fine.

"We'll give you a medal, Catfish."

"Nonsense," said the president.

"I know this cat.

 I've seen this cat before.

 He doesn't want a medal.

 What this Catfish wants is a

 bright, new, shiny

 very, very fast . . .

          AUTOMOBILE.

AND THAT'S WHAT HE'S GOING TO GET."